# THE WAITING SONG

Written by
Natasha Barber

Illustrated by
Rayah Jaymes

THE WAITING SONG

All marketing and publishing rights guaranteed to and reserved by:

**FUTURE HORIZONS** INC.

721 W. Abram St. Arlington, TX 76013

Toll-free: 800·489·0727 | Fax: 817·277·2270

www.FHautism.com | info@FHautism.com

ISBN: 9781941765562

This Book Belongs To

_____

# The Waiting Song

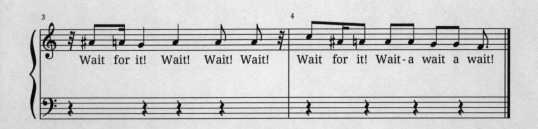

Nigel is a hedgehog. He's four years old, likes trains and cookies, and is a lot like other kids in class.

Nigel has autism. He doesn't talk or say many words. He learns some things fast and some things slowly. He flaps his hands and rocks his body back and forth when he gets very excited.

Nigel is not very good at taking turns or being polite,
and he really does not like to wait.

One day at school, Nigel saw Pablo with a toy truck
and tried to take it away from him.

Pablo pulled the truck back and yelled,

"MINE!"

Nigel screamed and ran away when he did not get the toy truck.
"Nobody wants to play with me!" cried Nigel.

His teacher, Miss Little said, "Nigel, you need to learn to wait your turn."

However, Nigel did not like to wait.

Pablo asked Miss Little, "Why does Nigel act so different! He's not fun to play with!"

Miss Little replied, "I know it's hard when people are different, Pablo, but we are all different in our own way. Nigel learns some things fast and some things slowly. We can all help teach Nigel to share and wait. If you let him, he just might teach you something, too."

9

At home, Nigel tried to take his brother's toy blocks.

Nevil pulled his blocks back and shouted,

# "MINE!"

Nigel screamed
and ran away.

"Nobody wants
to play with me!"

11

Nigel's mom said,

"Nigel, you need to learn to wait your turn."

"That doesn't sound very fun," he thought.

"What can I do while I wait so I won't be so bored?"

Nigel thought
and thought.
"I know!"
Nigel shouted.
"When I have
to wait, I can
sing a song."

14

"YOU---GOTTA---WAIT---WAIT---WAIT---WAIT---FOR---IT!
WAIT---WAIT---WAIT---WAIT---FOR---IT!
WAIT---A---WAIT---A---WAIT!"

The next day at school, Nigel really wanted to play with Charlie's toy train and reached for it.

Charlie pulled the train back and yelled, **"MINE!"**

Nigel did not scream or run away. He flapped his hands, rocked back and forth, and sang his waiting song.

"YOU---GOTTA---WAIT---WAIT---WAIT---WAIT---FOR---IT! WAIT---WAIT---WAIT---WAIT---FOR---IT! WAIT---A---WAIT---A---WAIT!"

Charlie saw how patiently Nigel waited and invited Nigel to play with him.

"Great job waiting, Nigel!" said Miss Little.

At the end of the school day, Miss Little thanked Charlie, "It takes Nigel a little longer to learn classroom rules, like waiting."

"Thank you for inviting him to play with you today. That was very kind."

19

At home, Nigel tried to take Nevil's toy soldiers away.

Nevil pulled his soldiers back and yelled, "MINE!"

Nigel did not scream or run away.
He flapped his hands, rocked back and forth,
and sang his waiting song.

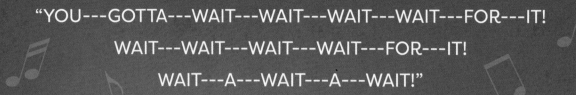

"YOU---GOTTA---WAIT---WAIT---WAIT---WAIT---FOR---IT!
WAIT---WAIT---WAIT---WAIT---FOR---IT!
WAIT---A---WAIT---A---WAIT!"

Nevil saw how patiently Nigel waited and said, "Nigel, let's play!"
"Great job waiting, Nigel!" said Nigel and Nevil's mom.

23

That night before he fell asleep, Nigel thought about what happened at school and at home when he waited his turn. "Learning to wait does help." "And I really like singing my new song."

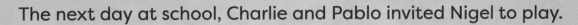

The next day at school, Charlie and Pablo invited Nigel to play.

"Nigel, do you want to play with us?" Pablo asked.

"You are good at waiting your turn," Charlie said.

"Did you know horses used to pull the first trains?"

"That is so cool!" said Pablo and Charlie,
while Nigel flapped his hands, rocked back and forth,
and hummed his waiting song.

Natasha Barber, the mother of a child on the autism spectrum, is the founder and manager of "Autism Moms Know Safety." She has written for numerous parenting blogs, including "Mobile Mommies" and "Paradigm Behavior," and she has had multiple safety articles featured in *Autism Parenting Magazine*. She is the author of the *Tommy's Lessons* children's book series. Books in this series include *My Tomato, Guacamole and Onion Sandwich*, *My Magic Pet Fish*, and *My Super Cool Ant Farm*.

Rayah Jaymes is an illustrator, chef, and musician. She comes from a large multicultural family which inspires her art, creativity, and storytelling. She has illustrated over 15 children's books and continues to write and illustrate books with a focus on humane education—teaching empathy, understanding, and respect for people, animals, and our environment. Her goal is to encourage children and their parents to learn about the diverse world around them and how they can make it better every day in everything they do. You can find more of Rayah's work at vcartist.com.

## Dedication

This book is dedicated to Joshua S., who is the inspiration for the main character Nigel and who came up with the waiting song during his therapy sessions while waiting for his iPad.

To Isaac S., Grayson B., and Zach B., Joshua's brothers who are so patient and helpful with their brother.

And, finally, to our dear friend Abby S., whose pet hedgehog Nigel was the perfect choice to represent Joshua.